A Note to Parents and Caregivers:

Read-it! Joke Books are for children who are moving ahead on the amazing road to reading. These fun books support the acquisition and extension of reading skills as well as a love of books.

Published by the same company that produces *Read-it!* Readers, these books introduce the question/answer pattern that helps children expand their thinking about language structure and book formats.

When sharing a book with your child, read in short stretches, pausing often to talk about the pictures and the meaning of the book. The question/answer format works well for this purpose and provides an opportunity to talk about the language and meaning of the jokes. Have your child turn the pages and point to the pictures and familiar words. Read the story in a natural voice; have fun creating the voices of characters or emphasizing some important words. And be sure to re-read favorite parts.

There is no right or wrong way to share books with children. Find time to read with your child and pass on the legacy of literacy.

Adria F. Klein, Ph.D.
Professor Emeritus
California State University
San Bernardino, California

Look for the other books in this series:
Animal Quack-Ups: Foolish and Funny Jokes About Animals (1-4048-0125-1)
Chewy Chuckles: Deliciously Funny Jokes About Food (1-4048-0124-3)
Dino Rib Ticklers: Hugely Funny Jokes About Dinosaurs (1-4048-0122-7)
Monster Laughs: Frightfully Funny Jokes About Monsters (1-4048-0123-5)
School Buzz: Classy and Funny Jokes About School (1-4048-0121-9)

Editor: Nadia Higgins
Designer: John Moldstad
Page production: Picture Window Books
The illustrations in this book were prepared digitally.

Picture Window Books
5115 Excelsior Boulevard
Suite 232
Minneapolis, MN 55416
1-877-845-8392
www.picturewindowbooks.com

Printed in the United States of America.
1 2 3 4 5 6 08 07 06 05 04 03

Library of Congress Cataloging-in-Publication Data
Dahl, Michael.
Galactic giggles : far-out and funny jokes about outer space /
written by Michael Dahl ; illustrated by Brandon Reibeling.
p. cm. — (Read-it! joke books)
Summary: An easy-to-read collection of jokes about astronauts,
stars, and other objects in space.
ISBN 1-4048-0126-X (library binding)
1. Outer space—Juvenile humor. 2. Wit and humor, Juvenile.
[1. Outer space—Humor. 2. Riddles. 3. Jokes.] I. Reibeling, Brandon,
ill. II. Title. III. Series.
PN6231.S645 D34 2003
818'.5402—dc21
                                                    2002156394

Galactic
Giggles

Far-Out and Funny Jokes
About Outer Space

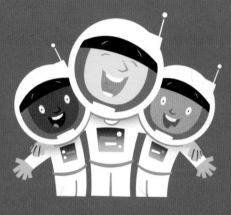

Michael Dahl • Illustrated by Brandon Reibeling

Reading Advisers:
Adria F. Klein, Ph.D.
Professsor Emeritus, California State University
San Bernardino, California

Susan Kesselring, M.A., Literacy Educator
Rosemount-Apple Valley-Eagan (Minnesota) School District

PiCTURE WiNDOW BOOKS
Minneapolis, Minnesota

How is a hockey player like a comet?

They are both shooting stars.

5

How do you get a baby astronaut to sleep?

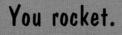

You rocket.

What kind of songs do astronauts sing?

Nep-tunes.

Where do astronauts leave their spaceships?

At parking meteors.

9

How did the rocket lose its job?

It got fired.

What did the astronauts make for dinner?

An unidentified frying object.

Why are astronauts
always so clean?

Because of all the meteor showers.   13

How do astronauts relax?

They read comet books.

What special dessert is found in every rocket ship?

An astronaut float.

How did the Martians serve dinner in outer space?

On flying saucers.

What is found at the center of Jupiter?

The letter *i*.

What do you call spacemen who tell lots of jokes?

Astronuts!

Where does the Martian president live?

What happened to the
astronomer when the
telescope fell on his head?

He saw stars.

23

What is an astronaut's favorite meal?

Launch.